The sergeant arst no questions, but 'e winked the other eye,
E' sez to me, "'Shun!" an' I shunted, the same as in days gone by;
For 'e saw the set o' my shoulders, an' I couldn't 'elp 'oldin' straight
When me an' the other rookies come under the barrick gate.

Back to the Army again, sergeant,
Back to the Army again;
'Oo would ha' thought I could carry an' port?
I'm back to the Army again!

I took my bath, an' I wallered—for, Gawd, I needed it so!
I smelt the smell o' the barricks, I 'eard the bugles go.
I 'eard the feet on the gravel—the feet o' the men what drill—
An' I sez to my flutterin' 'eartstrings, I sez to 'em, "Peace, be still!"

Back to the Army again, sergeant,
Back to the Army again;
'Oo said I knew when the Jumner was due?
I'm back to the Army again!

I carried my slops to the tailor; I sez to ' m, "None o' your lip!
You tight 'em over the shoulders, an' loose 'em over the 'ip,
For the set o' the tunic's 'orrid." An' 'e sez to me, "Strike me dead,
But I thought you was used to the busiress!" an' so 'e done what I said.

Back to the Army again, sergeant,
Back to the Army again.
Rather too free with my fancies? Wot—me?
I'm back to the Army again!

Next week I'll 'ave 'em fitted; I'll buy me a walkin' cane;
They'll let me free o' the barricks to walk on the Hoe again
In the name o' William Parsons, that used to be Edward Clay,
An'—any pore beggar that wants it can draw my fourpence a day!

Back to the Army again, sergeant,
Back to the Army again:
Out o' the cold an' the rain, sergeant,
Out o' the cold an' the rain.

'Oo's there?
A man that's too good to be lost you,
A man that is 'andled an' made—
A man that will pay what 'e cost you
In learnin' the others their trade—parade!
You're droppin' the pick o' the Army
Because you don't 'elp 'em remain,
But drives 'em to cheat to get out o' the street

An' back to the Army again!

"BIRDS OF PREY" MARCH

March! The mud is cakin' good about our trousies.
Front!—eyes front, an' watch the Colour-casin's drip.
Front! The faces of the women in the 'ouses
Ain't the kind o' things to take aboard the ship.

Cheer! An' we'll never march to victory.
Cheer! An' we'll never live to 'ear the cannon roar!
The Large Birds o' Prey
They will carry us away,
An' you'll never see your soldiers any more!

Wheel! Oh, keep your touch; we're goin' round a corner.
Time!—mark time, an' let the men be'ind us close.
Lord! the transport's full, an' 'alf our lot not on 'er—
Cheer, O cheer! We're going off where no one knows.

March! The Devil's none so black as 'e is painted!
Cheer! We'll 'ave some fun before we're put away.
'Alt, an' 'and 'er out—a woman's gone and fainted!
Cheer! Get on—Gawd 'elp the married men to-day!

Hoi! Come up, you 'ungry beggars, to yer sorrow.
('Ear them say they want their tea, an' want it quick!)
You won't have no mind for slingers, not to-morrow—
No; you'll put the 'tween-decks stove out, bein' sick!

'Alt! The married kit 'as all to go before us!
'Course it's blocked the bloomin' gangway up again!
Cheer, O cheer the 'Orse Guards watchin' tender o'er us,
Keepin' us since eight this mornin' in the rain!

Stuck in 'eavy marchin'-order, sopped and wringin'—
Sick, before our time to watch 'er 'eave an' fall,
'Ere's your 'appy 'ome at last, an' stop your singin'.
'Alt! Fall in along the troop-deck! Silence all!

Cheer! For we'll never live to see no bloomin' victory!
Cheer! An' we'll never live to 'ear the cannon roar! (One cheer more!)
The jackal an' the kite
'Ave an 'ealthy appetite,
An' you'll never see your soldiers any more! ('Ip! Urroar!)
The eagle an' the crow

They are waitin' ever so,
An' you'll never see your soldiers any more! ('Ip! Urroar!)
Yes, the Large Birds o' Prey
They will carry us away,
An' you'll never see your soldiers any more!

'SOLDIER AN' SAILOR TOO"

As I was spittin' into the Ditch aboard o' the Crocodile,
I seed a man on a man-o'-war got up in the Reg'lars' style.
'E was scrapin' the paint from off of 'er plates, an I sez to 'im, "'Oo are you?"
Sez 'e, "I'm a Jolly—'Er Majesty's Jolly—soldier an' sailor too!"
Now 'is work begins at Gawd knows when, and 'is work is never through;
'E isn't one o' the reg'lar Line, nor 'e isn't one of the crew.
'E's a kind of a giddy harumfrodite—soldier an' sailor too!

An' after I met 'im all over the world, a-doin' all kinds of things,
Like landin' 'isself with a Gatlin' gun to talk to them 'eathen kings;
'E sleeps in an 'ammick instead of a cot, an' 'e drills with the deck on a slew,
An' 'e sweats like a Jolly—'Er Majesty's Jolly—soldier an' sailor too!
For there isn't a job on the top o' the earth the beggar don't know, nor do.
You can leave 'im at night on a bald man's 'ead, to paddle 'is own canoe;
'E's a sort of a bloomin' cosmopolouse—soldier an' sailor too.

We've fought 'em on trooper, we've fought 'em in dock, an' drunk with 'em in betweens,
When they called us the seasick scull'ry maids, an' we called 'em the Ass Marines;
But, when we was down for a double fatigue, from Woolwich to Bernardmyo,
We sent for the Jollies—'Er Majesty's Jollies—soldier an' sailor too!
They think for 'emselves, an' they steal for 'emselves, and they never ask what's to do,
But they're camped an' fed an' they're up an' fed before our bugle's blew.
Ho! they ain't no limpin' procrastitutes—soldier an' sailor too.

You may say we are fond of an 'arness-cut, or 'ootin' in barrick-yards,
Or startin' a Board School mutiny along o' the Onion Guards;
But once in a while we can finish in style for the ends of the earth to view,
The same as the Jollies—'er Majesty's Jollies—soldier an' sailor too!
They come of our lot, they was brothers to us; they was beggars we'd met an' knew;
Yes, barrin' an inch in the chest an' the arms, they was doubles o' me an' you;
For they weren't no special chrysanthemums—so dier an' sailor too!

To take your chance in the thick of a rush, with firng all about,
Is nothing so bad when you've cover to 'and, an' leave an' likin' to shout;
But to stand an' be still to the Birken'ead drill is a damn tough bullet to chew,
An' they done it, the Jollies—'Er Majesty's Jollies—soldier an' sailor too!
Their work was done when it 'adn't begun; they was younger nor me an' you;
Their choice it was plain between drownin' in 'eaps an' bein' mashed by the screw,

So they stood an' was still to the Birken'ead drill, soldier an' sailor too!

We're most of us liars, we're 'arf of us thieves, an' the rest are as rank as can be,
But once in a while we can finish in style (which I 'ope it won't 'appen to me).
But it makes you think better o' you an' your friends, an' the work you may 'ave to do,
When you think o' the sinkin' Victorier's Jollies—soldier an' sailor too!
Now there isn't no room for to say ye don't know—they 'ave proved it plain and true—
That whether it's Widow, or whether it's ship, Victorier's work is to do,
An' they done it, the Jollies—'Er Majesty's Jollies—soldier an' sailor too!

SAPPERS

When the Waters were dried an' the Earth did appear
("It's all one," says the Sapper),
The Lord He created the Engineer,
Her Majesty's Royal Engineer,
With the rank and pay of a Sapper!

When the Flood come along for an extra monsoon,
'Twas Noah constructed the first pontoon
To the plans of Her Majesty's, etc.

But after "fatigue" in the wet an' the sun,
Old Noah got drunk, which he wouldn't ha' done
If he'd trained with, etc.

When the Tower o' Babel had mixed up men's bat,
Some clever civilian was managing that,
An' none of, etc.

When the Jews had a fight at the foot of an 'ill,
Young Joshua ordered the sun to stand still,
For he was a Captain of Engineers, etc.

When the Children of Israel made bricks without straw,
They were learnin' the regular work of our Corps,
The work of, etc.

For ever since then, if a war they would wage,
Behold us a-shinin' on history's page—
First page for, etc.

We lay down their sidings an' help 'em entrain,
An' we sweep up their mess through the bloomin' campaign,
In the style of, etc.

They send us in front with a fuse an' a mine
To blow up the gates that are rushed by the Line,
But bent by, etc.

They send us behind with a pick an' a spade,
To dig for the guns of a bullock-brigade
Which has asked for, etc.

We work under escort in trousies an' shirt,
An' the heathen they plug us tail-up in the dirt,
Annoying, etc.

We blast out the rock an' we shovel the mud,
We make 'em good roads an'—they roll down the khud,
Reporting, etc.

We make 'em their bridges, their wells, an' their huts,
An' the telegraph-wire the enemy cuts,
An' it's blamed on, etc.

An' when we return an' from war we would cease,
They grudge us adornin' the billets of peace,
Which are kept for, etc.

We build 'em nice barricks—they swear they are bad,
That our Colonels are Methodist, married or mad,
Insultin', etc.

They haven't no manners nor gratitude too,
For the more that we help 'em the less will they do,
But mock at, etc.

Now the Line's but a man with a gun in his hand,
An' Cavalry's only what horses can stand,
When helped by, etc.

Artillery moves by the leave o' the ground,
But we are the men that do something all round,
For we are, etc.

I have stated it plain, an' my argument's thus,
("It's all one," says the Sapper),
There's only one Corps which is perfect—that's us;
An' they call us Her Majesty's Engineers,
Her Majesty's Royal Engineers,
With the rank and pay of a Sapper!

THAT DAY

It got beyond all orders an' it got beyond all 'ope;
It got to shammin' wounded an' retirin' from the 'alt.
'Ole companies was lookin' for the nearest road to slope;
It were just a bloomin' knock-out—an' our fault!

Now there ain't no chorus 'ere to give,
Nor there ain't no band to play;
An' I wish I was dead 'fore I done what I did
Or seen what I seed that day!

We was sick o' bein' punished, an' we let 'em know it, too;
An' a company-commander up an' 'it us with a sword,
An' some one shouted "'Ook it!" an' it come to sove-ki-poo,
An' we chucked our rifles from us—oh, my Gawd!

There was thirty dead an' wounded on the ground we wouldn't keep—
No, there wasn't more than twenty when the front begun to go;
But, Christ! along the line o' flight they cut us up like sheep,
An' that was all we gained by doin' so.

I 'eard the knives be'ind me, but I dursn't face my man,
An' I don't know where I went to, 'cause I didn't 'alt to see,
Till I 'eard a beggar squealin' out for quarter as 'e ran,
An' I thought I knew the voice an'—it was me!

We was 'idin' under bedsteads more than 'arf a march away;
We was lyin' up like rabbits all about the country side;
An' the major cursed 'is Maker 'cause 'e lived to see that day,
An' the colonel broke 'is sword acrost, an' cried.

We was rotten 'fore we started—we was never disciplined;
We made it out a favour if an order was obeyed;
Yes, every little drummer 'ad 'is rights an' wrongs to mind,
So we had to pay for teachin'—an' we paid!

The papers 'id it 'andsome, but you know the Army knows;
We was put to groomin' camels till the regiments withdrew,
An' they give us each a medal for subduin' England's foes,
An' I 'ope you like my song—because it's true!

An' there ain't no chorus 'ere to give,
Nor there ain't no band to play;
But I wish I was dead 'fore I done what I did
Or seen what I seed that day!

A SONG OF INSTRUCTION

The men that fought at Minden, they was rookies in their time—
So was them that fought at Waterloo!
All the 'ole command, yuss, from Minden to Maiwand,
They was once dam' sweeps like you!

Then do not be discouraged, 'Eaven is your 'elper,
We'll learn you not to forget;
An' you mustn't swear an' curse, or you'll only catch it worse,
For we'll make you soldiers yet.

The men that fought at Minden, they 'ad stocks beneath their chins,
Six inch 'igh an' more;
But fatigue it was their pride, and they would not be denied
To clean the cook-'ouse floor.

The men that fought at Minden, they 'ad anarchistic bombs
Served to 'em by name of 'and-grenades;
But they got it in the eye (same as you will by an' by)
When they clubbed their field-parades.

The men that fought at Minden, they 'ad buttons up an' down,
Two-an'-twenty dozen of 'em told;
But they didn't grouse an' shirk at an hour's extry work,
They kept 'em bright as gold.

The men that fought at Minden, they was armed with musketoons,
Also, they was drilled by 'alberdiers;
I don't know what they were, but the sergeants took good care
They washed be'ind their ears.

The men that fought at Minden, they 'ad ever cash in 'and
Which they did not bank nor save,
But spent it gay an' free on their betters—such as me—
For the good advice I gave.

The men that fought at Minden, they was civil—yuss, they was—
Never didn't talk o' rights an' wrongs,
But they got it with the toe (same as you will get it—so!)—
For interrupting songs.

The men that fought at Minden, they was several other things
Which I don't remember clear;

But that's the reason why, now the six-year men are dry,
The rooks will stand the beer!

Then do not be discouraged, 'Eaven is your 'elper,
We'll learn you not to forget;
An' you mustn't swear an' curse, or you'll only catch it worse,
And we'll make you soldiers yet.

Soldiers yet, if you've got it in you—
All for the sake o' the Core;
Soldiers yet, if we 'ave to skin you—
Run an' get the beer, Johnny Raw—Johnny Raw!
Ho! run an' get the beer, Johnny Raw!

CHOLERA CAMP

We've got the cholerer in camp—it's worse than forty fights;
We're dyin' in the wilderness the same as Isrulites!
It's before us, an' be'ind us, an' we cannot get away,
An' the doctor's just reported we've ten more to-day!

Oh, strike your camp an' go, the bugle's callin',
The Rains are fallin'—
The dead are bushed an' stoned to keep 'em safe below;
The Band's a-doin' all she knows to cheer us;
The chaplain's gone and prayed to Gawd to 'ear us—
To 'ear us—
O Lord, for it's a-killing of us so!

Since August, when it started, it's been sticking to our tail,
Tho' they've 'ad us out by marches an' they've 'ad us back by rail;
But it runs as fast as troop-trains, an' we can not get away;
An' the sick-list to the Colonel makes ten more to-day.

There ain't no fun in women nor there ain't no bite to drink;
It's much too wet for shootin', we can only march and think;
An' at evenin', down the nullahs, we can 'ear the jackals say,
"Get up, you rotten beggars, you've ten more to-day!"

'Twould make a monkey cough to see our way o' doin' things—
Lieutenants takin' companies an' captains takin' wings,
An' Lances actin' Sergeants—eight file to obey—
For we've lots o' quick promotion on ten deaths a day!

Our Colonel's white an' twitterly—'e gets no sleep nor food,
But mucks about in 'orspital where nothing does no good.

'E sends us 'eaps o' comforts, all bought from 'is pay—
But there aren't much comfort 'andy on ten deaths a day.

Our Chaplain's got a banjo, an' a skinny mule 'e rides,
An' the stuff 'e says an' sings us, Lord, t makes us split our sides!
With 'is black coat-tails a-bobbin' to Ta-ra-ra Boom-der-ay!
'E's the proper kind o' padre for ten deaths a day.

An' Father Victor 'elps 'im with our Roman Catho icks—
He knows an 'eap of Irish songs an' rummy conjurin' tricks;
An' the two they works together wher it comes to play or pray;
So we keep the ball a-rollin' on ten deaths a day.

We've got the cholerer in camp—we've got it 'ot an' sweet;
It ain't no Christmas dinner, but it's 'elped an' we must eat.
We've gone beyond the funkin', 'cause we've found it doesn't pay,
An' we're rockin' round the Districk on ten deaths a day!

Then strike your camp an' go, the Rains are fallin',
The bugle's callin'!
The dead are bushed an' stoned to keep 'em safe below!
An' them that do not like it they can lump it,
An' them that can not stand it they can jump it;
We've got to die somewhere—some way—some'ow—
We might as well begin to do it now!
Then, Number One, let down the tent-pole slow,
Knock out the pegs an' 'old the corners—so!
Fold in the flies, furl up the ropes, an' stow!
Oh, strike—oh, strike your camp an' go!
(Gawd 'elp us!)

THE LADIES

I've taken my fun where I've found it;
I've rogued an' I've ranged in my time;
I've 'ad my pickin' o' sweet'earts,
An' four o' the lot was prime.
One was an 'arf-caste widow,
One was a woman at Prome,
One was the wife of a jemadar-sais,*
An' one is a girl at 'ome.

Now I aren't no 'and with the ladies,
For, takin' 'em all along,
You never can say till you've tried 'em,
An' then you are like to be wrong.

There's times when you'll think that you mightn't,
There's times when you'll know that you might;
But the things you will learn from the Yellow an' Brown,
They'll 'elp you an 'eap with the White!

I was a young un at 'Oogli,
Shy as a girl to begin;
Aggie de Castrer she made me,
An' Aggie was clever as sin;
Older than me, but my first un—
More like a mother she were—
Showed me the way to promotion an' pay,
An' I learned about women from 'er.

Then I was ordered to Burma,
Actin' in charge o' Bazar,
An' I got me a tiddy live 'eathen
Through buyin' supplies off 'er pa.
Funny an' yellow an' faithful—
Doll in a teacup she were,
But we lived on the square, like a true-married pair,
An' I learned about women from 'er.

Then we was shifted to Neemuch
(Or I might ha' been keepin' 'er now),
An' I took with a shiny she-devil,
The wife of a nigger at Mhow;
Taught me the gipsy-folks' bolee;**
Kind o' volcano she were,
For she knifed me one night 'cause I wished she was white,
And I learned about women from 'er.

Then I come 'ome in the trooper,
'Long of a kid o' sixteen—
Girl from a convent at Meerut,
The straightest I ever 'ave seen.
Love at first sight was 'er trouble,
She didn't know what it were;
An' I wouldn't do such, 'cause I liked 'er too much,
But—I learned about women from 'er!

I've taken my fun where I've found it,
An' now I must pay for my fun,
For the more you 'ave known o' the others
The less will you settle to one;
An' the end of it's sittin' and thinkin',
An' dreamin' Hell-fires to see;
So be warned by my lot (which I know you will not),

An' learn about women from me!

What did the colonel's lady think?
Nobody never knew.
Somebody asked the sergeant's wife,
An' she told 'em true.
When you get to a man in the case,
They're like as a row of pins—
For the colonel's lady an' Judy O'Grady
Are sisters under their skins!

*Head-groom.
**Slang.

BILL 'AWKINS

"'As anybody seen Bill 'Awkins?"
"Now 'ow in the devil would I know?"
"'E's taken my girl out walkin',
An' I've got to tell 'im so—
Gawd—bless—'im!
I've got to tell 'im so."

"D'yer know what 'e's like, Bill 'Awkins?"
"Now what in the devil would I care?"
"'E's the livin', breathin' image of an organ-grinder's monkey,
With a pound of grease in 'is 'air—
Gawd—bless—'im!
An' a pound o' grease in 'is 'air."

"An' s'pose you met Bill 'Awkins,
Now what in the devil 'ud ye do?"
"I'd open 'is cheek to 'is chin-strap buckle,
An' bung up 'is both eyes, too—
Gawd—bless—'im!
An' bung up 'is both eyes, too!"

"Look 'ere, where 'e comes, Bill 'Awkins!
Now what in the devil will you say?"
"It isn't fit an' proper to be fightin' on a Sunday,
So I'll pass 'im the time o' day—
Gawd—bless—'im!
I'll pass 'im the time o' day!"

THE MOTHER-LODGE

There was Rundle, Station Master,
An' Beazeley of the Rail,
An' 'Ackman, Commissariat,
An' Donkin o' the Jail;
An' Blake, Conductor-Sargent,
Our Master twice was 'e,
With 'im that kept the Europe shop,
Old Framjee Eduljee.

Outside—"Sergeant! Sir! Salute! Salaam!"
Inside—"Brother," an' it doesn't do no 'arm.
We met upon the Level an' we parted on the Square,
An' I was Junior Deacon in my Mother Lodge out there!

We'd Bola Nath, Accountant,
An' Saul the Aden Jew,
An' Din Mohammed, draughtsman
Of the Survey Office too;
There was Babu Chuckerbutty,
An' Amir Singh the Sikh,
An' Castro from the fittin'-sheds,
The Roman Catholick!

We 'adn't good regalia,
An' our Lodge was old an' bare,
But we knew the Ancient Landmarks,
An' we kep' 'em to a hair;
An' lookin' on it backwards
It often strikes me thus,
There ain't such things as infidels,
Excep', per'aps, it's us.

For monthly, after Labour,
We'd all sit down and smoke
(We dursn't give no banquits,
Lest a Brother's caste were broke),
An' man on man got talkin'
Religion an' the rest,
An' every man comparin'
Of the God 'e knew the best.

So man on man got talkin',
An' not a Brother stirred
Till mornin' waked the parrots
An' that dam' brain-fever-bird;
We'd say 'twas 'ighly curious,

An' we'd all ride 'ome to bed,
With Mo'ammed, God, an' Shiva
Changin' pickets in our 'ead.

Full oft on Guv'ment service
This rovin' foot 'ath pressed,
An' bore fraternal greetin's
To the Lodges east an' west,
Accordin' as commanded
From Kohat to Singapore,
But I wish that I might see them
In my Mother Lodge once more

I wish that I might see them,
My Brethren black an' brown,
With the trichies smellin' pleasant
An' the hog-darn* passin' down;
An' the old khansamah** snorin'
On the bottle-khana*** floor,
Like a Master in good standing
With my Mother Lodge once more!

Outside—"Sergeant! Sir! Salute! Salaam!"
Inside—"Brother," an' it doesn't do no 'arm.
We met upon the Level an' we parted on the Square,
An' I was Junior Deacon in my Mother Lodge out there!

*Cigar-lighter
**Butler
***Pantry

"FOLLOW ME 'OME"

There was no one like 'im, 'Orse or Foot,
Nor any o' the Guns I knew;
An' because it was so, why, o' course 'e went an' died,
Which is just what the best men do.

So it's knock out your pipes an' follow me!
An' it's finish up your swipes an' follow me!
Oh, 'ark to the big drum callin',
Follow me—follow me 'ome!

'Is mare she neighs the 'ole day long,
She paws the 'ole night through,
An' she won't take 'er feed 'cause o' waitin' for 'is step,

Which is just what a beast would do.

'Is girl she goes with a bombardier
Before 'er month is through;
An' the banns are up in church, for she's got the beggar hooked,
Which is just what a girl would do.

We fought 'bout a dog—last week it were—
No more than a round or two;
But I strook 'im cruel 'ard, an' I wish I 'adn't now,
Which is just what a man can't do.

'E was all that I 'ad in the way of a friend,
An' I've 'ad to find one new;
But I'd give my pay an' stripe for to get the beggar back,
Which it's just too late to do.

So it's knock out your pipes an' follow me!
An' it's finish off your swipes an' follow me!
Oh, 'ark to the fifes a-crawlin'!
Follow me—follow me 'ome!

Take 'im away! 'E's gone where the best men go.
Take 'im away! An' the gun-wheels turnin' slow.
Take 'im away! There's more from the place 'e come.
Take 'im away, with the limber an' the drum.

For it's "Three rounds blank" an' follow me,
An' it's "Thirteen rank" an' follow me;
Oh, passin' the love o' women,
Follow me—follow me 'ome!

THE SERGEANT'S WEDDIN'

'E was warned agin' 'er—
That's what made 'im look;
She was warned agin' 'im—
That is why she took.
Wouldn't 'ear no reason,
Went an' done it blind;
We know all about 'em,
They've got all to find!

Cheer for the Sergeant's weddin'—
Give 'em one cheer more!
Gray gun-'orses in the lando,

An' a rogue is married to, etc.

What's the use o' tellin'
'Arf the lot she's been?
'E's a bloomin' robber.
An' 'e keeps canteen.
'Ow did 'e get 'is buggy?
Gawd, you needn't ask!
Made 'is forty gallon
Out of every cask!

Watch 'im, with 'is 'air cut,
Count us filin' by—
Won't the Colonel praise 'is
Pop—u—lar—i—ty!
We 'ave scores to settle—
Scores for more than beer;
She's the girl to pay 'em—
That is why we're 'ere!

See the chaplain thinkin'?
See the women smile?
Twig the married winkin'
As they take the aisle?
Keep your side-arms quiet,
Dressin' by the Band.
Ho! You 'oly beggars,
Cough be'ind your 'and!

Now it's done an' over,
'Ear the organ squeak,
"Voice that breathed o'er Eden"—
Ain't she got the cheek
White an' laylock ribbons,
Think yourself so fine!
I'd pray Gawd to take yer
'Fore I made yer mine!

Escort to the kerridge,
Wish 'im luck, the brute!
Chuck the slippers after—
[Pity 'taint a boot!]
Bowin' like a lady,
Blushin' like a lad—
'Oo would say to see 'em—
Both are rotten bad!

Cheer for the Sergeant's weddin'—

Give 'em one cheer more!
Gray gun-'orses in the lando,
An' a rogue is married to, etc.

THE JACKET

Through the Plagues of Egyp' we was chasin' Arabi,
Gettin' down an' shovin' in the sun;
An' you might 'ave called us dirty, an' you might ha' called us dry,
An' you might 'ave 'eard us talkin' at the gun.
But the Captain 'ad 'is jacket, an' the jacket it was new—
('Orse-Gunners, listen to my song!)
An' the wettin' of the jacket is the proper thing to do,
Nor we didn't keep 'im waiting very long!

One day they give us orders for to shell a sand redoubt,
Loadin' down the axle-arms with case;
But the Captain knew 'is dooty, an' he took the crackers out,
An' he put some proper liquor in its place.
An' the Captain saw the shrapnel (which is six-an'-thirty clear).
('Orse-Gunners, listen to my song!)
"Will you draw the weight," sez 'e, "or will you draw the beer?"
An' we didn't keep 'im waitin' very long.

For the Captain, etc.

Then we trotted gentle, not to break the bloomin' glass,
Though the Arabites 'ad all their ranges marked;
But we dursn't 'ardly gallop, for the most was bottled Bass,
An' we'd dreamed of it since we was disembarked.
So we fired economic with the shells we 'ad in 'and,
('Orse-Gunners, listen to my song!)
But the beggars under cover 'ad the impidence to stand,
An' we couldn't keep 'em waitin' very long.

And the Captain, etc.

So we finished 'arf the liquor (an' the Captain took champagne),
An' the Arabites was shootin' all the while;
An' we left our wounded 'appy with the empties on the plain,
An' we used the bloomin' guns for pro-jec-tile!
We limbered up an' galloped—there were nothin' else to do—
('Orse-Gunners, listen to my song!)
An' the Battery come a-boundin' like a boundin' kangaroo,
But they didn't watch us comin' very long.

As the Captain, etc.

We was goin' most extended—we was drivin' very fine,
An' the Arabites were loosin' 'igh an' wide,
Till the Captain took the glassy with a rattlin' right incline,
An' we dropped upon their 'eads the other side.
Then we give 'em quarter—such as 'adn't up and cut,
('Orse-Gunners, listen to my song!)
An' the Captain stood a limberful of fizzy—somethin' Brutt,
But we didn't leave it fizzing very long.

For the Captain, etc.

We might ha' been court-martialled, but it all come out all right
When they signalled us to join the main command.
There was every round expended, there was every gunner tight,
An' the Captain waved a corkscrew in 'is 'and!
But the Captain had 'is jacket, etc.

THE 'EATHEN

The 'eathen in 'is blindness bows down to wood an' stone;
'E don't obey no orders unless they is 'is own;
'E keeps 'is side-arms awful: 'e leaves 'em all about,
An' then comes up the regiment an' pokes the 'eathen out.

All along o' dirtiness, all along o' mess,
All along o' doin' things rather-more-or-less,
All along of abby-nay,* kul,** and hazar-ho,***
Mind you keep your rifle an' yourself jus' so!

The young recruit is 'aughty—'e draf's from Gawd knows where;
They bid 'im show 'is stockin's an' lay 'is mattress square;
'E calls it bloomin' nonsense—'e doesn't know, no more—
An' then up comes 'is company an' kicks 'em round the floor!

The young recruit is 'ammered—'e takes it very 'ard;
'E 'angs 'is 'ead an' mutters—'e sulks about the yard;
'E talks o' "cruel tyrants" 'e'll swing for by-an'-bye,
An' the others 'ears an' mocks 'im, an' the boy goes orf to cry.

The young recruit is silly—'e thinks o' suicide;
'E's lost 'is gutter-devil; 'e 'asn't got 'is pride;
But day by day they kicks 'im, which 'elps 'im on a bit,
Till 'e finds 'isself one mornin' with a full an' proper kit.

Gettin' clear o' dirtiness, gettin' done with mess,
Gettin' shut o' doin' things rather-more-or-less;
Not so fond of abby-nay, kul, nor hazar-ho,
Learns to keep 'is rifle an' 'isself jus' so!

The young recruit is 'appy—'e throws a chest to suit;
You see 'im grow mustaches; you 'ear 'im slap 'is boot;
'E learns to drop the "bloodies" from every word he slings,
An' 'e shows an 'ealthy brisket when 'e strips for bars an' rings.

The cruel tyrant sergeants they watch 'im 'arf a year;
They watch 'im with 'is comrades, they watch 'im with 'is beer;
They watch 'im with the women, at the regimental dance,
And the cruel tyrant sergeants send 'is name along for "Lance."

An' now 'e's 'arf o' nothin', an' all a private yet,
'Is room they up an' rags 'im to see what they will get;
They rags 'im low an' cunnin', each dirty trick they can,
But 'e learns to sweat 'is temper an' 'e learns to know 'is man.

An', last, a Colour-Sergeant, as such to be obeyed,
'E leads 'is men at cricket, 'e leads 'em on parade;
They sees 'em quick an' 'andy, uncommon set an' smart,
An' so 'e talks to orficers which 'ave the Core at 'eart.

'E learns to do 'is watchin' without it showin' plain;
'E learns to save a dummy, an' shove 'im straight again;
'E learns to check a ranker that's buyin' leave to shirk;
An' 'e learns to make men like 'im so they'll learn to like their work.

An' when it comes to marchin' he'll see their socks are right,
An' when it comes to action 'e shows 'em 'ow to sight;
'E knows their ways of thinkin' and just what's in their mind;
'E feels when they are comin' on an' when they've fell be'ind.

'E knows each talkin' corpril that leads a squad astray;
'E feels 'is innards 'eavin', 'is bowels givin' way;
'E sees the blue-white faces all tryin' 'ard to grin,
An' 'e stands an' waits an' suffers till it's time to cap 'em in.

An' now the hugly bullets come peckin' through the dust,
An' no one wants to face 'em, but every beggar must;
So, like a man in irons which isn't glad to go,
They moves 'em off by companies uncommon stiff an' slow.

Of all 'is five years' schoolin' they don't remember much
Excep' the not retreatin', the step an' keepin' touch.
It looks like teachin' wasted when they duck an' spread an' 'op,

But if 'e 'adn't learned 'em they'd be all about the shop!

An' now it's "'Oo goes backward?" an' now it's "'Oo comes on?"
An' now it's "Get the doolies," an' now the captain's gone;
An' now it's bloody murder, but all the while they 'ear
'Is voice, the same as barrick drill, a-shepherdin' the rear.

'E's just as sick as they are, 'is 'eart is like to split,
But 'e works 'em, works 'em, works 'em till 'e feels 'em take the bit;
The rest is 'oldin' steady till the watchful bugles play,
An' 'e lifts 'em, lifts 'em, lifts 'em through the charge that wins the day!

The 'eathen in 'is blindness bows down to wood an' stone;
'E don't obey no orders unless they is 'is own;
The 'eathen in 'is blindness must end where 'e began,
But the backbone of the Army is the noncommissioned man!

Keep away from dirtiness—keep away from mess.
Don't get into doin' things rather-more-or-less!
Let's ha' done with abby-nay, kul, an' hazar-ho;
Mind you keep your rifle an' yourself jus' so!

*Not now
**To-morrow
***Wait a bit

THE SHUT-EYE SENTRY

Sez the Junior Orderly Sergeant
To the Senior Orderly Man:
"Our Orderly Orf'cer's hokee-mut,
You 'elp 'im all you can.
For the wine was old and the night is cold,
An' the best we may go wrong,
So, 'fore 'e gits to the sentry-box,
You pass the word along."

Then it was "Rounds! What rounds?" at two of a frosty night,
'E's 'oldin' on by the sergeant's sash, but, sentry, shut your eye.
An' it's "Pass! All's well!" Oh, ain't 'e rock n' tight!
'E'll need an affidavit pretty badly by-an'-bye.

The moon was white on the barricks,
The road was white an' wide,
An' the Orderly Orf'cer took it all,
An' the ten-foot ditch beside.

An' the corporal pulled an' the sergeant pushed,
An' the three they wagged along,
But I'd shut my eyes in the sentry-box,
So I didn't see nothin' wrong.

Though it was "Rounds! What rounds?" O corporal, 'old 'im up!
'E's usin' 'is cap as it shouldn't be used, but, sentry, shut your eye.
An' it's "Pass! All's well!" Ho, shun the foamin' cup!
'E'll need, etc.

'Twas after four in the mornin';
We 'ad to stop the fun,
An' we sent 'im 'ome on a bullock-cart,
With 'is belt an' stock undone;
But we sluiced 'im down an' we washed 'im out,
An' a first-class job we made,
When we saved 'im smart as a bombardier
For six o'clock parade.

It 'ad been "Rounds! What rounds?" Oh, shove 'im straight again!
'E's usin' 'is sword for a bicycle, but, sentry, shut your eye.
An' it was "Pass! All's well!" 'E's called me "darlin' Jane"!
'E'll need, etc.

The drill was 'ard an' 'eavy,
The sky was 'ot an' blue,
An' 'is eye was wild an' 'is 'air was wet,
But 'is sergeant pulled 'im through.
Our men was good old trusties—
They'd done it on their 'ead;
But you ought to 'ave 'eard 'em markin' time
To 'ide the things 'e said!

For it was "Right flank—wheel!" for "'Alt, an' stand at ease!"
An' "Left extend!" for "Centre close!" O marker, shut your eye!
An' it was, "'Ere, sir, 'ere! before the colonel sees!"
So he needed affidavits pretty badly by-an'-bye.

There was two-an'-thirty sergeants,
There was corp'rals forty-one,
There was just nine 'undred rank an' file
To swear to a touch o' sun.
There was me 'e'd kissed in the sentry-box
(As I 'ave not told in my song),
But I took my oath, which were Bible truth,
I 'adn't seen nothin' wrong.

There's them that's 'ot an' 'aughty,

There's them that's cold an' 'ard,
But there comes a night when the best gets tight,
An' then turns out the Guard.
I've seen them 'ide their liquor
In every kind o' way,
But most depends on makin' friends
With Privit Thomas A.

When it is "Rounds! What rounds?" 'E's breathin through 'is nose.
'E's reelin', rollin', roarin' ripe, but, sentry, shut your eye.
An' it's "Pass! All's well!" An' that's the way it goes.
We'll 'elp 'im for 'is mother, an' 'e'll 'elp us by-an'-bye.

"MARY, PITY WOMEN!"

You call yourself a man,
For all you used to swear,
An' leave me, as you can,
My certain shame to bear?
I 'ear! You do not care—
You done the worst you know.
I 'ate you, grinnin' there....
Ah, Gawd, I love you so!

Nice while it lasted, an' now it is over—
Tear out your 'eart an' good-bye to your lover!
What's the use o' grievin', when the mother that bore you
(Mary, pity women!) knew it all before you?

It aren't no false alarm,
The finish to your fun;
You—you 'ave brung the 'arm,
An' I'm the ruined one;
An' now you'll off an' run
With some new fool in tow.
Your 'eart? You 'aven't none....
Ah, Gawd, I love you so!

When a man is tired there is naught will bind 'im;
All 'e solemn promised 'e will shove be ind 'im.
What's the good o' prayin' for The Wrath to strike 'im,
(Mary, pity women!) when the rest are like 'im?

What 'ope for me or—it?
What's left for us to do?
I've walked with men a bit,

But this—but this is you!
So 'elp me Christ, it's true!
Where can I 'ide or go?
You coward through an' through!...
Ah, Gawd, I love you so!

All the more you give 'em the less are they for givin'!
Love lies dead, an' you can not kiss 'im livin'.
Down the road 'e led you there is no returnin',
(Mary, pity women!) but you're late in learnin'.

You'd like to treat me fair?
You can't, because we're pore?
We'd starve? What do I care!
We might, but this is shore:
I want the name—no more—
The name, an' lines to show,
An' not to be an 'ore....
Ah, Gawd, I love you so!

What's the good o' pleadin', when the mother that bore you
(Mary, pity women!) knew it all before you?
Sleep on 'is promises an' wake to your sorrow,
(Mary, pity women!) for we sail to-morrow!

FOR TO ADMIRE

The Injian Ocean sets an' smiles
So sof', so bright, so bloomin' blue;
There aren't a wave for miles an' miles
Excep' the jiggle from the screw.
The ship is swep', the day is done,
The bugle's gone for smoke an' play;
An' black agin' the settin' sun
The Lascar sings, "Hum deckty hai!"*

For to admire an' for to see,
For to be'old this world so wide—
It never done no good to me,
But I can't drop it if I tried!

I see the sergeants pitchin' quoits,
I 'ear the women laugh an' talk,
I spy upon the quarter-deck
The orficers an' lydies walk.
I thinks about the things that was,

An' leans an' looks acrost the sea,
Till, spite of all the crowded ship,
There's no one lef' alive but me.

The things that was which I 'ave seen,
In barrick, camp, an' action too,
I tells them over by myself,
An' sometimes wonders if they're true;
For they was odd—most awful odd—
But all the same now they are o'er,
There must be 'eaps o' plenty such,
An' if I wait I'll see some more.

Oh, I 'ave come upon the books,
An' often broke a barrick rule,
An' stood beside an' watched myself
Be'avin' like a bloomin' fool.
I paid my price for findin' out,
Nor never grutched the price I paid,
But sat in Clink without my boots,
Admirin' 'ow the world was made.

Be'old a cloud upon the beam,
An' 'umped above the sea appears
Old Aden, like a barrick-stove
That no one's lit for years an' years!
I passed by that when I began,
An' I go 'ome the road I came,
A time-expired soldier-man
With six years' service to 'is name.

My girl she said, "Oh, stay with me!"
My mother 'eld me to 'er breast.
They've never written none, an' so
They must 'ave gone with all the rest—
With all the rest which I 'ave seen
An' found an' known an' met along.
I cannot say the things I feel,
But still I sing my evenin' song:
For to admire an' for to see,
For to be'old this world so wide—
It never done no good to me,
But I can't drop it if I tried!

*"I'm looking out"

L'ENVOI

When Earth's last picture is painted, and the tubes are twisted and dried,
When the oldest colours have faded, and the youngest critic has died,
We shall rest, and, faith, we shall need it—lie down for an æon or two,
Till the Master of All Good Workmen shall set us to work anew!

And those that were good shall be happy: they shall sit in a golden chair;
They shall splash at a ten-league canvas with brushes of comets' hair;
They shall find real saints to draw from—Magdalene, Peter, and Paul;
They shall work for an age at a sitting and never be tired at all!

And only the Master shall praise us, and only the Master shall blame;
And no one shall work for money, and no one shall work for fame;
But each for the joy of the working, and each, in his separate star,
Shall draw the Thing as he sees It for the God of Things as They Are!

Rudyard Kipling – A Short Biography

Born in Bombay on 30th December 1865, Joseph Rudyard Kipling wrote short stories, poems and novels, a body of work whose reputation is in constant flux as his presentations and interpretations of empire are viewed within the changing context of empirical absolution in the twentieth century. Having spent the first five years of his life in India he felt a natural affinity for the country, though his upbringing had distinctly colonial taste flavour. He was born in the Bombay Presidency of British India to Lockwood Kipling, an English art teacher and illustrator who took a position as professor of architectural sculpture in the Jeejeebhoy School of Art and Alice MacDonald, spoken of by the a Viceroy of India that "dullness and Mrs Kipling cannot exist in the same room". Though their presence in India was principally artistic and educational, rather than political, the company they kept and the establishments in which they kept it indicate an existence very much benefitting from the British Empire. Lockwood would later go on to assume a position as curator of the Lahore Museum, while working on various illustrations for Rudyard' writing, and various decorations for the Victoria and Albert museum in London. Much of his work, then, was coloured by the empire, whether in service to or benefitting from, and it was into this distinctly British experience of India that Rudyard was born.

Lockwood and Alice had met and fallen in love at Rudyard Lake in Rudyard, Staffordshire, and their affections for the area were so great they chose to refer to the lake in naming their first-born. Alice came from a family of four sisters, all of whose marriages were significant and well-arranged; moreover Rudyard's most famous relative was Stanley Baldwin, Conservative Prime Minister on three occasions in the 1920s and 1930s. Kipling's sense of belonging in Bombay is found in 'To the City of Bombay' in the dedication to Seven Seas, a collection of poems published in 1900, which reads:—

> Mother of Cities to me,
> For I was born in her gate,
> Between the palms and the sea,
> Where the world-end steamers wait.

The Phantom 'Rickshaw and other Eerie Tales (1888)
Wee Willie Winkie and Other Child Stories (1888)
Life's Handicap (1891)
The Light that Failed (1891) (novel)
American Notes (1891) (non-fiction)
The Naulahka: A Story of West and East (1892) (with Wolcott Balestie)
Many Inventions (1893)
The Jungle Book (1894)
Mowgli's Brothers (short story)
Kaa's Hunting (short story)
Tiger! Tiger! (short story)
The White Seal (short story)
Rikki-Tikki-Tavi (short story)
Toomai of the Elephants (short story)
Her Majesty's Servants (originally titled Servants of the Queen) (short story)
The Second Jungle Book (1895)
How Fear Came (short story)
The Miracle of Purun Bhagat (short story)
Letting in the Jungle (short story)
The Undertakers (short story)
The King's Ankus (short story)
Quiquern (short story)
Red Dog" (short story)
The Spring Running (short story)
Captains Courageous (1896) (novel)
The Day's Work (1898)
A Fleet in Being (1898)
Stalky & Co. (1899)
From Sea to Sea and Other Sketches, Letters of Travel (1899) (non-fiction)
Kim (1901) (novel)
Just So Stories for Little Children (1902)
Traffics and Discoveries (1904) (24 collected short stories)
With the Night Mail (1905) A Story of 2000 A.D
Puck of Pook's Hill (1906)
The Brushwood Boy (1907)
Actions and Reactions (1909)
A Song of the English (1909) (with W. Heath Robinson illustrator)
Rewards and Fairies (1910)
A History of England (1911) (non-fiction with Charles Robert Leslie Fletcher)
Songs from Books (1912)
As Easy as A.B.C. (1912) (Science-fiction short story)
The Fringes of the Fleet (1915) (non-fiction)
Sea Warfare (1916) (non-fiction)
A Diversity of Creatures (1917)
Land and Sea Tales for Scouts and Guides (1923)
The Irish Guards in the Great War (1923) (non-fiction)
Debits and Credits (1926)
A Book of Words (1928) (non-fiction)

Thy Servant a Dog (1930)
Limits and Renewals (1932)
Tales of India: the Windermere Series (1935)
Something of Myself (1937) (autobiography)
The Elephant's Child (fiction)

Autobiographies and Speeches
A Book of Words (1928)
Something of Myself (1937)

Short Story Collections
Quartette (1885) – with his father, mother, and sister
Plain Tales from the Hills (1888)
Soldiers Three, The Story of the Gadsbys, In Black and White (1888)
The Phantom 'Rickshaw and other Eerie Tales (1888)
Under the Deodars (1888)
Wee Willie Winkie and Other Child Stories (1888)
Life's Handicap (1891)
Many Inventions (1893)
The Jungle Book (1894)
The Second Jungle Book (1895)
The Day's Work (1898)
Life's Handicap (1899)
Stalky & Co. (1899)
Just So Stories (1902)
Traffics and Discoveries (1904)
Puck of Pook's Hill (1906)
Actions and Reactions (1909)
Abaft the Funnel (1909)
Rewards and Fairies (1910)
The Eyes of Asia (1917)
A Diversity of Creatures (1917)
Land and Sea Tales for Scouts and Guides (1923)
Debits and Credits (1926)
Thy Servant a Dog (1930)
Limits and Renewals (1932)

Military Collections
A Fleet in Being (1898)
France at War (1915)
The New Army in Training (1915)
Sea Warfare (1916)
The War in the Mountains (1917)
The Graves of the Fallen (1919)
The Irish Guards in the Great War (1923)

www.ingramcontent.com/pod-product-compliance
Lightning Source LLC
Chambersburg PA
CBHW021941170626
46807CB00007B/3224

* 9 7 8 1 7 8 7 8 0 6 1 7 7 *